nickelodeon

GOOD PO, BAD PO

adapted by Natalie Shaw

Simon Spotlight
New York London Toronto Sydney New Delhi

SIMON SPOTLIGHT
An imprint of Simon & Schuster Children's Publishing Division
1230 Avenue of the Americas, New York, New York 10020
Kung Fu Panda Legends of Awesomeness © 2014 Viacom International Inc.
NICKELODEON and all related logos are trademarks of
Viacom International Inc. Based on the feature film "Kung Fu Panda" © 2008 DreamWorks
Animation L.L.C. All Rights Reserved. All rights reserved, including the right of reproduction in whole or in part
in any form. SIMON SPOTLIGHT and colophon are registered trademarks of Simon & Schuster, Inc.
For information about special discounts for bulk purchases, please contact Simon & Schuster Special Sales at
1-866-506-1949 or business@simonandschuster.com.
Manufactured in the United States of America 0615 LAK 10 9 8 7 6 5 4 3 2 1
ISBN 978-1-4814-4816-1   ISBN 978-1-4814-0002-2 (eBook)

Po was having a great day. He had just gotten a new kite, and he couldn't wait to fly it.

"Come on, kite. Up! Up, kitey, kitey, kitey," Po coaxed.

Soon the kite caught the wind and took Po—upside down—along for the ride.

"This . . . is . . . so . . . bodaciously . . . ah-ah-awesome!" Po yelled.

Just then Po heard fighting coming from the Jade Palace. It sounded like his friends were in trouble.

"Hang on, guys, I'm coming!" Po shouted, steering the kite toward the Jade Palace.

"I'm here!" Po announced upon his arrival. Seconds later someone threw Monkey at him. "All right. Who threw this?"

One of the warriors raised his hand.
"Buddy, you just made my list," said Po.
"Uh, what list?" the warrior asked.
"My list of people I'm going to hit really hard!" Po replied.

Po fought the warriors. Soon their leader, Temutai, was the only one left.

Temutai towered above Po. "You have bested my minions, Dragon Warrior. But you cannot defeat Temutai, Warrior-King of the Qidan!" he threatened.

"I beat you last time," Po countered. He ducked out of the way every time Temutai threw a punch.

Then Po spun around and threw a punch at Temutai . . . who was halfway across the room. Green light traveled from Po's paw and hit Temutai hard, blasting him through the wall of the Jade Palace!

"Panda," Shifu began, "where did you learn the Thundering Wind Hammer?" Po looked confused. "That thing I just did? Uh . . . I thought I made it up."

"It is one of the legendary Seven Impossible Moves! No one has done that since . . . since . . ." Shifu paused. "Well, never mind."

"Since what? The invention of bodacity?" Po laughed. Then he stuck out his hand to Monkey, hoping for a high five.

"Aah!" yelled Monkey. "Oh, no thanks! Maybe later! I, uh . . . hurt my hand!"

"High five anyone?" Po asked.

Everyone made an excuse and ran away. The high five looked just like the Thundering Wind Hammer move Po had used on Temutai.

"Okay, why's everyone acting so weird?" Po asked Shifu, who was the only one left.

Shifu explained that in the past there had been other Furious Fives. "Fenghuang the owl was the greatest fighter of us all. But she . . . changed. Over the years, the most powerful of us have become in a word: evil. And Po, you are the most powerful."

"Wh-what?" Po stuttered. "So that means . . . *I'm going to turn evil?*"

Po went to Monkey to find out more.

Monkey explained that Oogway, the leader of the old Furious Five, had trained Fenghuang to use her very special skills.

"She was the most powerful of the Five," Monkey said. "And that's when she started to change."

"Fenghuang challenged Oogway to fight, declaring that she would be master of the Jade Palace," Monkey went on. "But Oogway had been expecting this. He had built an inescapable, owl-shaped cage. He would have to defeat Fenghuang to get her into it. She could not defeat Oogway, but she could run. There's a rumor that she's been up in the Northern Mountains, too afraid of Oogway to return."

"And now everyone thinks that I'm going to go bad just like she did?" Po asked.

"What? No, of course not! Don't be silly," Monkey said nervously. He knocked down a folding screen, revealing . . .

"Is that a Panda-shaped cage?" Po asked.
Monkey denied it, but Po could see that it was.

Shifu told the others to treat Po like they always had, that Po wasn't evil yet, but they were already scared of him.

It was too much for Po.

"I'm not evil," Po said to his friends. "But I have decided that before I become a hideous, evil monster, I will leave the Valley of Peace forever. Don't try to stop me!"

And no one did.

Po left the Jade Palace, said good-bye to his father, and headed to the mountains with a very heavy heart.

After walking, walking, and more walking, Po became so tired he fell right down on his face. When he looked up, he saw an owl.

"You . . . you must be Fenghuang!" Po exclaimed. "I had to leave the Jade Palace before I hurt them. Before I became like you. Evil."

Fenghuang took Po back to her cave. "Who told you I was evil?" she asked. "Was it Oogway?"

"No," replied Po without thinking. "Shifu told me. Oogway is gone."

"Oogway is . . . gone?" Fenghuang cackled with glee. "Without Oogway, I can assume my rightful place as ruler of the Jade Palace! Come with me now, Po. We will return to the Jade Palace and annihilate everyone that you once loved."

"No!" yelled Po. "That's why I left. So I wouldn't hurt them. I can't let you go!"

Po and Fenghuang began to fight.

Soon they had fought their way to the edge of the cliff.

"You're good, Panda, but you can't win," said Fenghuang.

"Why not?" asked Po.

"Because I cheat!" With that, Fenghuang stepped off the edge of the cliff and flew away. "You'll come around and join me. Sooner than you think."

Fenghuang arrived at the Jade Palace, ready to fight.

"Shifu, you don't seem glad to see me," she mocked him as they battled. "If Oogway couldn't beat me, what chance do you have? It's time to say good-bye."

Just then they heard yelling. "Yeah! Bringing it from the sky!" Po said, landing in the Jade Palace. He had built a kite to escape Fenghuang's cave!

Fenghuang thought Po was coming to join her.

"No, I've come back to stop you," Po corrected her. "So in my last moments of not-yet-evil, I say KEEE-YA!"

While Po and Fenghuang fought for the second time that day, Fenghuang used other Impossible Moves that Po had never seen before.

"Want to learn the Mongolian Fireball?" Fenghuang demonstrated it. "I can teach you all of the Seven Impossible Moves."

Po repeated the Mongolian Fireball perfectly.

Po agreed with Fenghuang. "We are the most powerful. We should rule . . . and we will."

With that, he turned and grabbed Shifu!

"Have you lost your mind?" Shifu asked.

"No! I came to my senses!" Po replied.

When Fenghuang came up to congratulate him, Po . . .

trapped her in the owl-shaped cage.

"Wow, it still fits you perfectly after all these years!" Po said.

Fenghuang was stunned. "You actually took out Shifu just so you could sneak up on me?"

Po nodded happily and informed Fenghuang of the rest of his plan. "You're going to Chor Ghom prison. Don't worry. It's actually nicer than your old place."

Everyone was amazed at what Po had done, and that he hadn't become evil.

"I'm not going to turn evil," Po announced. "Turns out it's only happened to the strongest member of the Furious Five. I'm not one of the Furious Five! No Dragon Warrior has ever turned evil!"

"So, you want me to get rid of that panda-shaped cage?" Monkey quietly asked Shifu.

"Um . . . no," Shifu said. "Better safe than sorry."

But they all knew that Po was good inside, and that he always would be.